The Adventures of
Davey Prickle
by
Chris Shea

for Gigi,
Finn
and
Ryan

and dedicated to Jeanine,
the strongest soft person
I know...

In a gentle little corner of a great big desert, there lived a small green cactus named
Davey Prickle.

Davey lived along a sandy, dry river bed lined on either side with beautiful weeds. He loved the warm desert sun and the way the sky rested above him like an upside down bowl.

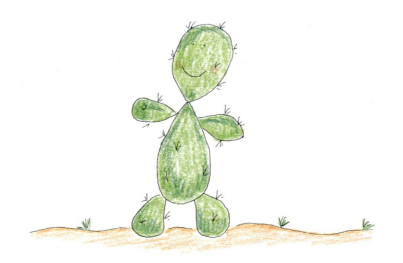

But Davey mostly loved his two best friends:
Hiss, a garden variety green snake
and
Sissy, a garden variety green hose
(who thought she was a snake, too!)

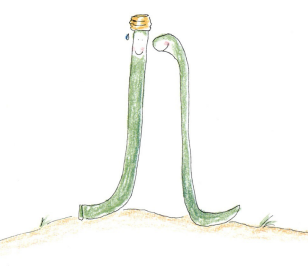

Early one summer afternoon, Davey, Hiss,
and Sissy were enjoying a little Neapolitan
ice cream when a soft desert breeze blew
an invitation onto Davey's stickery toe.
    It read,

            Summer Dance Tonight
            Bring a snack to share
            Dance the night away
               7:00 PM Sharp !

"A dance!" cried Davey with joy. He picked up Hiss and danced around in circles.
"Ouch!!" Hiss complained loudly. "Your stickers hurt! Put me down."
"But I love to dance," said Davey.
"Then you'll need a partner who's prickly like you," Sissy pointed out.

But Davey had no stickery friends.
All his friends were smooth.
Or fuzzy.
Or soft and slimy.
They would all say "ouch!"
    "I wish that I were soft," said Davey
Prickle sadly. "Then someone would dance
with me."

Then Sissy had a great idea. "Maybe Hiss and I could make you soft! We could cover you with cotton balls so your stickers wouldn't hurt whoever you were dancing with."

"Hmm..." said Davey Prickle thoughtfully. "Could you really make me soft?"

"Of course we can," said Sissy. "And I know exactly where to go: to the Weevil Drug and Sundries Store across the river bed at the Desert Mall."

Davey paused to imagine how he'd look all covered in cotton balls: kind of silly! But he didn't care.

"Okay, I'll do it," he announced.

"Then we've got work to do," said Sissy. "You've got to go clean up, and we've got to get to the mall."

So Davey, Hiss and Sissy said their good-byes and headed off in opposite directions.

Hiss and Sissy started out as clouds began to darken above their heads.

"I hope it doesn't rain," Hiss said.

But it did seem awfully dark to them, so they decided to change their plans. Instead of taking the pathway home after they left the mall, they'd take a little short cut home along the bottom of the dry river bed.

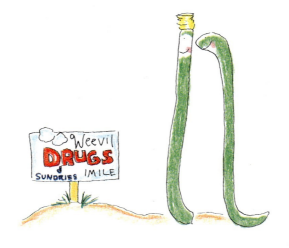

After Davey got back home, he started getting ready for the dance. He took a thirty minute watermelon-pomegranate bubble bath. He brushed his pearly teeth and combed his spiky hair. His heart was singing. He was so excited!

Then Davey looked into his mirror at the Davey looking back.

"I imagine we'll have lots of fun," he said picturing the evening ahead...

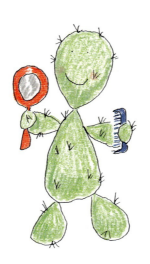

He soon began to daydream. He thought about the snacks to share, because Davey loved to eat! And he thought about the music, especially the drums.

"My daydream drums are really loud," he said, and then he gasped,

"Oh No!"

For it wasn't drumming he imagined. It was thunder. And it was <u>real</u>!

Hiss and Sissy started running when the rain began to fall. But so much water came so fast, the two friends and their cotton box began floating down the quickly filling river.

"Let's paddle over to that rock until this storm has passed," yelled Hiss to Sissy as they rafted on the little box.

"Poor Davey," they said softly as they climbed up on the rock. "We'll never get the cotton there in time."

From his backyard Davey Prickle watched
the river rise. His hopes for dancing fell.
His heart sank as he thought about his
friends, because he knew they must be
stranded somewhere in the storm.

"But what if," he began to wonder,
"they've already got the cotton and they're
waiting at the dance for me..."

... So Davey quickly put a smile on his
face and some macaroons in a little brown
bag. Then he put his raincoat on and
headed out the door.
"I can't let Hiss and Sissy down,
in case they're waiting there."

Davey hurried to the dance in the pouring rain. Once there he looked everywhere. But all he saw were dancers and none of them were Sissy. Not one of them was Hiss.

"I guess I won't be dancing," he whispered to himself. "Not tonight at least I won't." Then he tried hard not to cry.

But there was more to do that night than dance. There were snacks and treats! (And remember, Davey loved to eat.)
So Davey put his macaroons out on the "TREATS FOR SHARING TABLE." Then he chose a delicious piece of chocolate cake and a cup of kiwi punch. After only three little bites and two tiny sips, he started feeling better. He even started smiling!

Next, Davey folded up his raincoat and placed it on the floor beneath the little crimson wooden bench he sat on all alone. "I can have fun anyway!" he reassured himself.

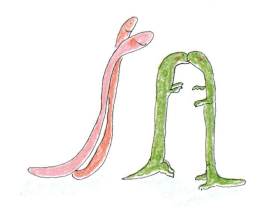

Davey ate a little more cake as two pink snakes danced by. Then he saw two lizards kiss and he closed his eyes and sighed.

"If only I were soft. Then I know someone would dance with me."

But Davey Prickle wasn't soft, so he sat and sat and sat. No one asked him if he'd like to dance, and those he asked said "no."

From seven o'clock until nine-fifteen,
Davey was a very good sport. But finally,
by half-past nine the disappointed little
cactus decided he'd go home.
    He recycled his napkin, plate and paper
cup and wiped six crumbs off his stickery
chin. As he turned to take a final look at the
dancers dancing by, he ran right into
someone who was coming in the door!
    Her name was Lacey Staple. She
reached to shake Davey's prickly hand hello.

"You didn't say ouch," he said amazed. "Everybody does, you know, when they shake my hand or even just accidentally touch my arm."

"Oh stickers don't hurt me even one little bit. I'm a cotton plant, you know."

"Cotton?" asked Davey, who could not believe his ears.

"Yes," she smiled. "And the best part of being cotton is that I can dance with anyone, even cactus boys like you!"

"You mean, you'd really dance with me?"

"Of course! I'd be delighted," came Lacey's kind reply. Then she took Davey by the hand and walked to the center of the room.

"Look! That little cactus fellow is finally going to dance," said one snake to another. Soon everyone began to clap and cheer for Davey as the band played a merry song. His dream was really coming true.

At last, Davey Prickle got to dance!

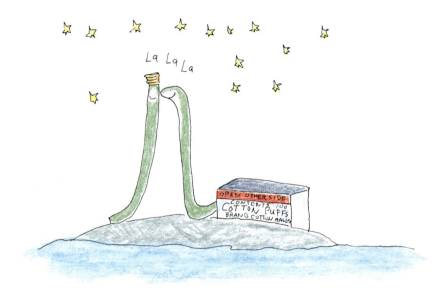

Now, Hiss and Sissy had a feeling Davey would be having fun, so they weren't sad there on their rock. Instead they laughed and sang and watched the stars dance by.

"The water will be gone by morning," a sleepy Sissy said.

"Then we'll just wait here safe and sound," yawned a drowsy Hiss. And then he fell asleep.

Even though the invitation said the dance
began at seven, it didn't seem quite like that to
Davey. For him the dance really didn't start
until Lacey Staple said,
  "Of course! I'd be delighted."
She was soft enough for two...

So Davey danced with Lacey Staple
to his heart's content. He brought her
macaroons. They drank cold punch and
watched the stars (the same stars Hiss
and Sissy watched!) and danced and
danced some more.

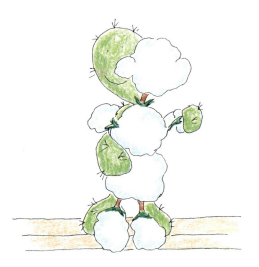

hello!

In fact they had so much fun dancing,
they didn't even hear the music stop.
So even when the sun came up, it found
them dancing still...

The End